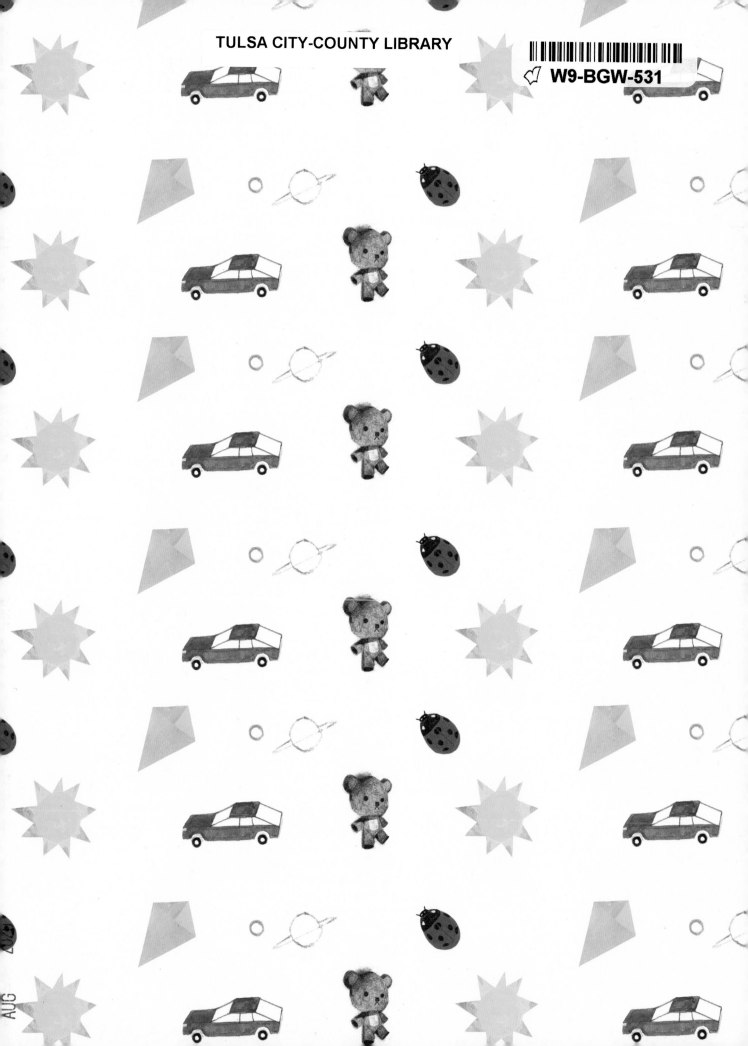

For Samuel, Georgia, and Isaac
and their wondrous ways
—K.A.H.

To Kirsten, always in wonder
—K.P.

Text copyright © 2019 by Kari Anne Holt
Jacket art and interior illustrations copyright © 2019 by Kenard Pak

All rights reserved. Published in the United States by Random House Children's Books,
a division of Penguin Random House LLC, New York.

Random House and the colophon are registered trademarks of Penguin Random House LLC.

Visit us on the Web!
rhcbooks.com

Educators and librarians, for a variety of teaching tools, visit us at RHTeachersLibrarians.com

Library of Congress Cataloging-in-Publication Data is available upon request.
ISBN 978-1-5247-1422-2 (trade) — ISBN 978-1-5247-1423-9 (lib. bdg.) —
ISBN 978-1-5247-1424-6 (ebook)

MANUFACTURED IN CHINA
10 9 8 7 6 5 4 3 2
First Edition

i wonder

Words by K. A. Holt
Pictures by Kenard Pak

Random House
New York

What if the sun is really a kite?

Is cereal afraid of the spoon?

I wonder if sandwiches get
mad when you bite them.

What if the ocean is one big water bottle?

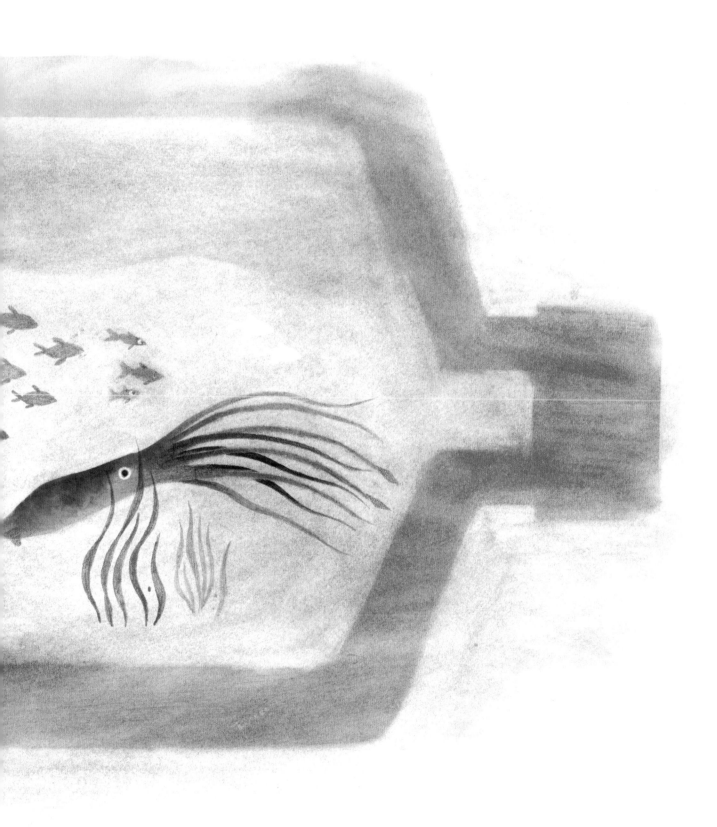

Do tires get tired?

I wonder if dragonflies dog-paddle.

Do bubbles tickle everything they touch?

Is a fly a baby in the morning
and an old man at night?

Does a grasshopper take hopping lessons?

I wonder if cars and trucks
speak the same language.

Do windmills ever get tired?

Where are all the unicorns hiding?

I wonder if boy ladybugs
are called boybugs.

What do clouds taste like?

Do my toys miss me when I'm gone?

How does a clock know what time it is?

I wonder if shoes feel sad when
they don't fit me anymore.

Could there be a galaxy
in my belly button?

I wonder if books read us, too.

What do stars do during the day?

Is wind made or born?

Do trees have dreams?

I wonder if teddy bears ever cry.

Why don't shadows smile when you smile?

I wonder how tomorrow
knows how to get here.

I wonder why I wonder so much.

Because you are wonderful.

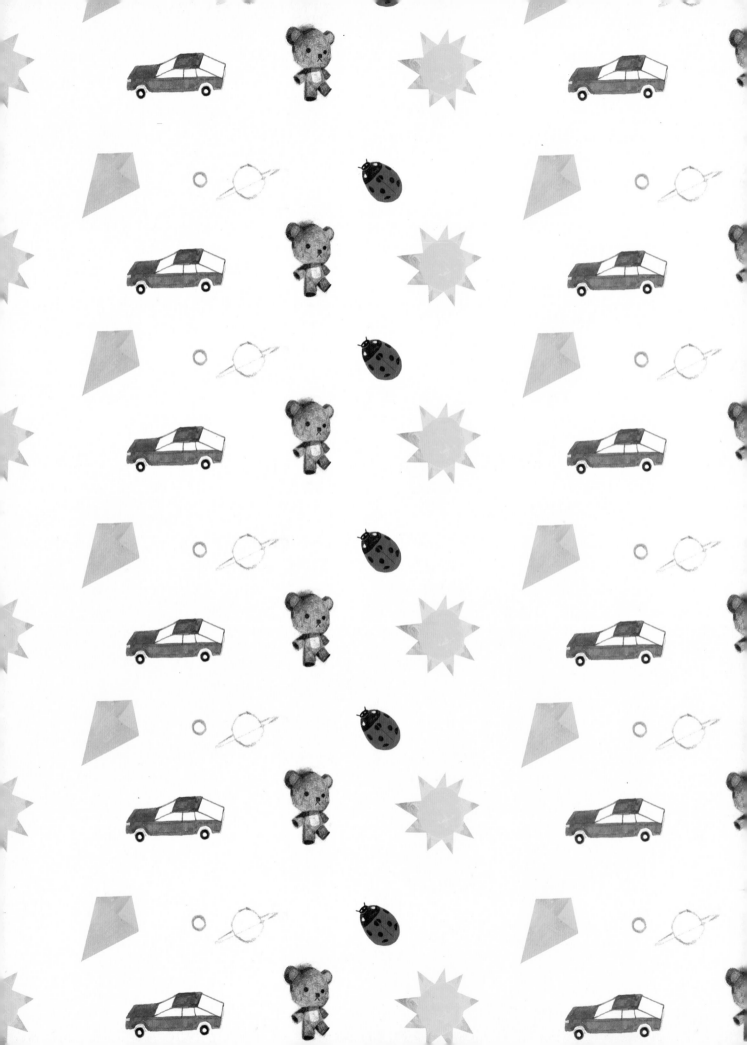